Rhino, Rhino, Sweet Potato

For Emilia
–F. P.

For my mom
–M.S.A.

Rhino, Rhino, Sweet Potato
Text copyright © 2009 by Francine Prose
Illustrations copyright © 2009 by Matthew S. Armstrong
Manufactured in China.

Library of Congress Cataloging-in-Publication Data
Prose, Francine.
    Rhino, rhino, sweet potato / by Francine Prose ; illustrated by Matthew S. Armstrong. — 1st ed.
        p.   cm.
    Summary: When hungry rhinos rampage the village eating all the sweet potatoes, Roy bravely goes and teaches them new
ways to live.
    ISBN 978-0-06-008078-5 (trade bdg.) — ISBN 978-0-06-008079-2 (lib. bdg.)
    [1. Stories in rhyme. 2. Rhinoceroses—Fiction. 3. Plants—Fiction. 4. Courage—Fiction.] I. Armstrong, Matthew (Matthew
S.), 1975– ill. II. Title.
PZ8.3.P93655Rh 2009   2008010084
[E]—dc22   CIP
                                                                                                                                  AC

Typography by Matt Adamec 1 2 3 4 5 6 7 8 9 10 ❖ First Edition

Rhino, Rhino, Sweet Potato

Francine Prose

illustrated by

Matthew S. Armstrong

HarperCollinsPublishers

In a village far away
Lived a little boy.
The name of the village was Sweet Potato.
Our hero's name was Roy.

The way their village got its name
Everybody knew.
Sweet potatoes were what they ate.
Sweet potatoes were what they grew.

Sweet potato dumplings, sweet potato pies,
Sweet potato noodles, sweet potato fries,
Sweet potatoes on the grill, sweet potato ice,
Sweet potato candy, sweet potato rice.

They farmed the sweet potato patch
All the warm day long.
And while they worked, they sang
This sweet potato song:

Sweet potato, we love you,
Sweet potato big and tall.
Sweet potato summer, sweet potato fall,
Sweet potato January, sweet potato June.
Sweet potato, hear our happy little tune.
Sweet potato fat and strong,
Sweet potato dear.
Sweet potato, feed us
All sweet potato year.

One night while Sweet Potato slept,
A rumbling rocked their beds.
A roar like a thousand freight trains
Shook the sleep from their heads.

Roy ran to his window.
What was the racket about?
He heard the sound of hoofbeats.
He heard his neighbors shout,
"Rhino rampage! Look out!"

Roy began to shiver.
He knew a herd of rhinoceros
Lived just across the river.

The rhinos had never crossed before.
The water was deep and cold.
The rhinos liked to snooze in the sun.
The rhinos were never so bold.

But now the hungry rhinos
Dug up the plants and went on
Eating every potato,
Till every potato was gone.

At last the rhinos turned around
And swam back across the stream,
Leaving the frightened villagers
To wonder if it was a dream.

Only the torn-up leaves and vines
In the sweet potato field
Proved that it was no nightmare.
The runaway rhinos were real.

Sweet Potato held a meeting
To decide what to do.
Everyone in town was there.
Roy attended, too.

Everybody talked at once,
Till finally someone said,
"The next time the rhinos come to our town,
We'll shoot those rhinos dead!"

But Roy stood up and shouted, with a tear in his eye,
"Wait! I have another plan so the rhinos don't have to die."
Some people said, "He's only a boy."
But others said, "Let him try."

By the light of the moon Roy took a canoe
And rowed from shore to shore,
Singing a brave little song to himself
As he lifted and pulled the oar.

Roy began to sing louder
To keep his shaking hands still.
And the rhinos began to listen,
As even rhinos will,
When a song is clear and true
And sung straight from the heart.
Roy sang all the way to the end of the song,
Then sang it again from the start.

Rhino, rhino, sweet potato,
Sweet potato pie.
Rhino, baby rhino,
Rhino, don't you cry.
Rhino, don't you worry.
Rhino, don't you weep.
Rhino, rhino, sweet potato,
Rhino baby, sleep.

Roy sang his song again and again,
Trembling all the while
Until he was almost sure
He saw the rhinos smile.
Until the rhinos waved their horns
And did a silly dance,
Stumbling and skipping rhinos
In a happy trance.

In the bottom of the boat
Were several enormous sacks.
Roy lifted them and placed them
On the rhinos' backs.

He led the herd of rhinos
To a place where there were no trees.
He patiently showed the rhinos
How to get down on their knees.
How to use their horns to dig in the ground
And root out the brambles and weeds.

Roy reached down into his sack,
All the while singing his song,
And took the baby sweet potato
Plants he'd brought along.

He laid the plants in straight rows
And covered them with sand.
Then climbed back in his canoe
And rowed away from land.

From time to time, when the weather got dry,
Roy rowed across once more
And taught the rhinos to carry water
From the river shore.

Together they tended and watered the plants
Till the sweet potatoes grew high.
And each time Roy sang the rhinos
His rhino lullaby:

Rhino, rhino, sweet potato,
Sweet potato pie.
Rhino, baby rhino,
Rhino, don't you cry.
Rhino, don't you worry.
Rhino, don't you weep.
Rhino, rhino, sweet potato,
Rhino baby, sleep.

Now on one side of the river
The rhinos eat what they've grown.
And nowadays on the other side
The villagers have their own:

Sweet potato dumplings, sweet potato pies,
Sweet potato noodles, sweet potato fries,
Sweet potatoes on the grill, sweet potato ice,
Sweet potato candy, sweet potato rice.

Now everyone has sweet potatoes
And everyone sings Roy's song.
And sometimes it even seems to Roy
That the rhinos sing along:

Rhino, rhino, sweet potato,
Sweet potato pie.
Rhino, baby rhino,
Rhino, don't you cry.
Rhino, don't you worry.
Rhino, don't you weep.
Rhino, rhino, sweet potato,
Rhino baby, sleep.